This book belongs to:

*To Vinson Ming-Da, my precious kite flier;
to Greg, the wind beneath my kite.*
—Y.C.C.

*To my papercut and kites master, Guo Cheng Yi.*
—Y.X.

Immedium, Inc.
P.O. Box 31846
San Francisco, CA 94131
www.immedium.com

First hardcover edition published 2003 by Holiday House.
First Immedium hardcover edition published 2016.

Book design by Joy Liu-Trujillo for Swash Design Studio
Chinese translation by Venus Chow and Carissa Duan

中文审校：张瀛、邹海燕

Printed in Malaysia
10 9 8 7 6 5 4 3 2 1

Library of Congress Cataloging-in-Publication Data

Compestine, Ying Chang.
The story of kites / by Ying Chang Compestine ; illustrated by YongSheng Xuan. —1st ed.
p. cm.
Summary: Long ago in China, three brothers become tired of chasing birds from their family's rice
fields and experiment with ways to make the job easier.
ISBN: 0-8234-1715-8 (hardcover)
[1. Brothers—Fiction. 2. Farm life—China—Fiction. 3. Kites—Fiction. 4. China—History—Fiction.]
I. Xuan, YongSheng, ill. II. Title: PZ7.C73615 Ste 2003
[Fic]—dc21
2002027375

ISBN: 978-1-59702-122-7

# The Story of Kites

## Amazing Chinese Inventions

# 风筝的故事
### 神奇的中国发明

By **Ying Chang Compestine** · 张瀛/文
Illustrated by **Yongsheng Xuan** · 宣永生/图

immedium

Immedium, Inc.   San Francisco

**Long ago in China,** children worked in the rice fields during the harvest season. The three Kang boys — Ting, Pan, and Kùai — marched through the fields, blew whistles, and banged pots and pans to scare away the birds. *Tweeeeee! Bang!! Klang!!!* Pan stopped banging. "I need a break to do my math homework."

"Why do the birds always eat our rice?" Ting asked.

"Because they're hungry like me! If I had wings, I would chase these birds away in the sky."

Just as Kùai picked up his noodle bowl, a gust of wind whisked away the boys' straw hats, homework, and chopsticks. They ran after their things.

**在很久以前的中国，**每当丰收的季节，孩子们都会在稻田里干活。康家三兄弟——廷、盼和快，在地里一边吹着口哨走着，一边敲着锅碗瓢盆驱赶鸟儿。哔——！呼！哐！盼不敲了，他说："我要停会儿，去做数学作业了。"

廷问道："为什么那些鸟老是来吃我们的稻子呢？"

"因为它们和我一样饿了！如果我有翅膀的话，我就会飞到天上把这些鸟赶走。"

快刚端起面碗，一阵大风把他们的草帽、作业本和筷子都吹走了。男孩们在后面追跑着。

When they caught up with their things, Ting asked, "Did you see how high my hat flew? We can make wings with straw."

"My homework stayed up longer," said Pan. "Paper is lighter."

"I would use feathers," Kùai said thoughtfully.

A month later on a windy spring day, the boys climbed the hill near their village. Each wore a set of wings.

Ting's were made of woven straw. Pan's were made of paper and bamboo chopsticks. Kùai made the biggest with chicken feathers.

当他们追到时，廷问："你们看到我的帽子飞得有多高吗？我们可以用稻草做一双翅膀。"

"我的作业本飞得更高，"盼说。"因为纸更轻。"

"我会用羽毛來做翅膀。"快若有所思地说。

一个月后，在一个风和日丽的春日，男孩们爬上村旁的山上。
每人都背着一双翅膀。

廷的翅膀是用稻草编的。盼的翅膀是用纸和竹筷造的。快用鸡毛拼成的翅膀最大。

"Ready... set... FLY!" yelled Kùai.

The boys jumped.

They flapped their wings. But they all went in one direction... down.

*Kersplash! Kerplop! Kersploosh!* They landed right in the middle of the rice field.

"What's happening?" cried a farmer. "Did rocks just fall off the hill?"

"Did a chicken just fall from the sky?" asked a lady.

"Did a straw hat make that noise?" asked an old man.

The villagers quickly gathered around.

"各就各位，预备……一、二、三……飞！"快大叫。

男孩们跳起来。他们拍动翅膀……但他们都往下坠。

呱唧！扑腾！哗啦！他们跌落在稻田中心。

一个农夫喊道："出什么事了？石头从山上掉下来了吗？"

一个农妇问："是不是有只鸡从天上掉下来了？"

一个老人问："刚刚那声音是草帽发出的吗？"

村民们很快地聚集在周围。

When the Kang boys emerged from the mud, even their parents couldn't recognize them.

"Oh, my wings," groaned Kùai.

"I told you chickens can't fly," said Ting, dragging his straw wings out of the mud.

"You should have used bird feathers," said Pan, yanking at his shredded paper-chopstick wings.

All the villagers started laughing, even Mama and Papa.

当康家兄弟从泥里爬出来的时候，连他们的父母也没认出他们。

"噢，我的翅膀。"快呻吟道。

"我告诉过你没有会飞的鸡。"廷边说边从泥里拖出他的稻草翅膀。

"你应该用鸟儿的羽毛。"盼边说边拽着他那撕破了的用纸和竹筷做的翅膀。

村民们都笑了起来，妈妈和爸爸也笑了。

After a long bath, Kùai said, "I wonder where I can find enough bird feathers to make new wings."

"I am not doing it again," said Ting. "My mouth still tastes like mud and my arms hurt."

"Me neither," agreed Pan. "And I didn't like it when everyone laughed at us."

Ignoring his brothers' complaints, Kùai said, "We're too heavy for wings, but I have another idea."


洗过澡后，<u>快</u>说："我不知道去哪儿可以找到足够的鸟羽毛来做新翅膀。"

"我不想再干了，"<u>廷</u>说。"我嘴里还有泥巴味，我的胳膊也疼。"

"我也不干了，"<u>盼</u>同意。"我不喜欢被人取笑。"

<u>快</u>不理兄弟们的抱怨，说："我们太重了，翅膀带不动我们，但是我还有一个主意。"

The next day, the three boys painted scary faces on their straw hats and waited. Soon a strong wind swept through and blew their hats right into a flock of birds. The birds fled from the scary faces. The boys jumped up and down, cheering.

When the wind died down, the hats were nowhere to be found... but Pan's homework was still flying.

That night, the boys had to help unhappy Papa make new straw hats. "We can't fly our hats again. It will upset Papa," said Pan.

第二天，三个男孩在草帽上画上狰狞的面孔，并在稻田里等候着。不一会儿，一阵强风把他们的帽子吹到鸟群中。鸟儿慌忙逃开那吓人的面孔。男孩们欢呼雀跃。

风停后，帽子找不到了……但<u>盼</u>的作业本还在飞。

那天晚上，男孩们只好帮生气的爸爸编织新草帽。"我们不能让帽子再飞走了，爸爸会不高兴的。"<u>盼</u>说。

"But I wouldn't mind losing my math homework." Ting smiled mischievously.

"And I like losing my chopsticks so I don't have to wash them," Kùai giggled.

"但我不在乎弄丢我的数学作业本。"廷淘气地笑了。

快咯咯地笑着说："我就想弄丢我的筷子，这样我就不用洗了。"

A few days later, a new set of wings made from bamboo chopsticks and homework sailed up into the sky. The boys tied long strings to the wings to prevent them from flying away.

The wings startled the birds for a while. But they soon grew used to them and ignored the wings.

几天后, 用竹筷和作业本做的新翅膀飞上天了。男孩们在翅膀上栓了一根长长的绳子, 以防它们飞走。

鸟一开始都被那些翅膀吓到了, 但很快就习惯了, 不再理睬。

"Boys!" yelled Mama. "The birds are eating our rice! Keep blowing and banging!"

"We need to make our wings scarier." Kùai started banging on a pot.

"I know what we can do!" Pan picked up a whistle.

"I have an idea too," said Ting.

"Fine, let's see who can scare the birds away," said Kùai.


"儿子们！"妈妈叫道。"鸟在吃我们的稻子！继续吹，继续敲！"

"我们得做更吓人的翅膀。"快开始敲锅。

"我知道我们该怎样做了！"盼拿起哨子。

"我也有一个主意。"廷说。

"好吧，我们看谁能把鸟吓走。"快说。

Two weeks later, the boys returned to the hill above the rice fields. Each held something big in his hands.

"Look, the Kang boys are going to fly again," one villager yelled.

"You mean jump into the rice fields?" said another.

"Oh dear, they are wearing their nice clothes," Mama exclaimed. "Papa, quick, go stop..."

Before Mama could finish her sentence, the three boys had let go of what was in their hands.

两个星期后，男孩们回到山上。每人都拿着一件大东西。

一个村民喊道："看，康家的孩子们又要飞了。"

另一个村民说："你是说他们要跳到田里去吗？"

妈妈惊呼："天呐，那是过节穿的衣服。孩子他爸，快去阻止……"

妈妈还没说完，男孩们已经放开了手中的东西。

Ting launched a colorful phoenix with a long tail. Pan released a blue butterfly. Kùai tossed up a dark bird with a bamboo flute tied underneath. The tail of the phoenix danced around in the gentle breeze, and the butterfly's wings flapped up and down.

All the villagers gathered around. "What are those?"

"Look, the dark bird is singing!"

"Ho, the wind is playing the dark bird's flute!"

"The birds all flew away!"

廷放了一只色彩缤纷的带着长尾巴的凤凰。盼放了一只蓝色的蝴蝶。快抛起了一只黑色的鸟，下面绑着一只竹笛。凤凰的尾巴在和风中舞动，蝴蝶的翅膀在上下拍动。

所有村民都围过来。"那是什么？"

"瞧，那只黑鸟在唱歌！"

"啊，风在吹奏绑在黑鸟上的笛子！"

"鸟都飞走了！"

Mama and Papa ran up the hill and the villagers followed. They saw that the boys had tied their inventions to a tree, and were laughing and eating Long-Life Noodles.

"What are those things in the sky?" asked an old man.

Kùai stood up and said, "They are meant to scare away the birds, so we don't have to blow whistles or bang pots and pans anymore."

"What are they called?" asked another villager.

妈妈和爸爸往山上跑，村民们在后面跟着。他们看到男孩们把发明物绑在树上，一边笑，一边吃着长寿面。

一个老人问道："天上飞的是什么？"

<u>快讯速</u>站起来说："那是用来吓鸟的，这样我们就不用吹哨子或敲锅盆了。"

另一个村民问："那些东西叫什么？"

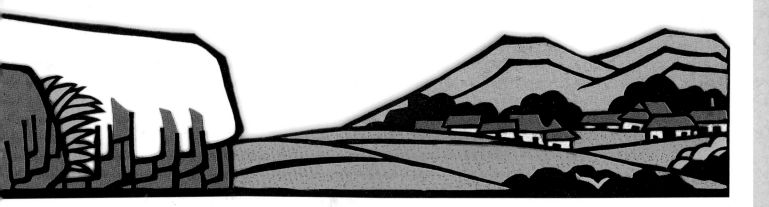

Ting and Pan looked at Kùai.

"Since they make music that sounds like the strings of the zheng, I call them *fengzheng* — wind *zheng* — kites."

"You have to teach us how to make them!" said the old man.

廷和盼看着快。

"因为这些东西会发出像筝弦一样的声音，我就叫它风筝。"

"你一定要教我们怎样做这些风筝！"老人说。

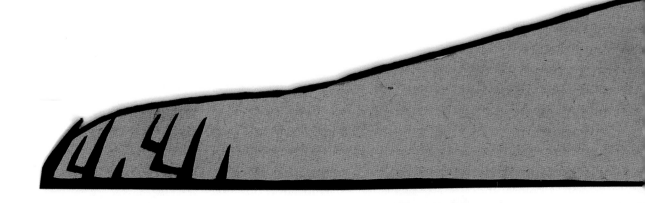

The Kang family opened the very first kite factory in China. They made kites of all colors and shapes. Better yet, no more birds came to eat their village's rice, because the sky was full of kites — dragons, fish, flying tigers, and phoenixes.

康家开办了中国第一家风筝厂。他们制做不同颜色和形状的风筝。令人欣慰的是，因为天上到处都飞着龙、鱼、飞虎和凤凰的风筝，再也没有鸟儿去吃村里的稻子了。

# Author's Note

Kites originated in China. An ancient Chinese philosopher, Mo Di, flew a kite 2,400 years ago, which may have been one of the first in the world. Later, the kite spread to other Asian countries and from there, around the globe.

There is no exact record of how or why the kite was invented. A common theory suggests that it was inspired either by the wind blowing a straw hat or by flying birds. Because the Chinese believed the soul was like a flying bird, the kite was especially symbolic. A flying kite would scare evil out of the sky and protect the soul.

Today in China, people celebrate festivals with kites. During the spring Festival of the Lantern and the fall Festival of Climbing Heights, kites are flown throughout the country, generally from high ground.

There are many varieties of kites. Some bear small candle lanterns, while others carry fireworks to set off high in the sky. Among the most impressive kites are musical ones. One type of kite dangles mussel shells that make a rattling sound in the wind, while another type has a drum and a cymbal at the top. Still other kites carry bamboo flutes that sound like harps in the wind.

The wind plays these kites like a musician playing a never-ending lullaby on a *zheng*, a Chinese stringed instrument. This led to the Chinese name *fengzheng* meaning "wind *zheng*," as the Kang boys call their invention.

## How to Fly a Kite:

1. Try to stand on high ground, such as a hill. Plan where you are going to run before launching your kite.

2. Standing with your back to the wind, hold the kite in the air. When the wind blows, let go of the kite. Turn and run as fast as you can into the wind. When you feel the wind tug at the kite, release some of the string. Let the wind do the job for you. Each time you feel a tug, let out more of your string. You will get better with practice.

# Homemade Diamond Kite

With the help of an adult, you can make your own kite by following the steps below.

## You will need:

- Two long sticks or homemade chopsticks. Have an adult help you cut the sticks, so that one stick is about two-thirds the length of the other (i.e. 12 and 18 inches)

- A small knife
- A roll of string
- Scissors
- Glue or softly cooked rice

- A big piece of paper — try using newspaper, white paper, or your old math homework!
- A marker

## Directions:

1. Center the short stick one-third of the way down the longer stick to make a cross.

2. Secure the two sticks together by tying a piece of string around the joints three times, crossing both ways. Tie it with a knot. A dab of glue will help secure the knot.

3. Have an adult notch the ends of each stick with the knife.

4. Starting at the bottom of the longer stick and moving clockwise, slot a piece of string into all four notches, pulling the string tight all the way around to make a diamond shape. The string ends should meet at the bottom of the longer stick. Secure the string there with a double knot. You can trim off the remaining string or leave a length for the tail.

5. Lay the frame over your paper. Mark around the edges where you will cut the paper, leaving a 1-inch margin outside the string frame.

6. After cutting out the paper, spread glue all around the edges where the frame will rest. Press the frame gently onto the paper. Fold the edges of the paper over the string of the frame.

7. To make the bridle, which is the loop of string on a kite that attaches the frame to the line, cut a piece of string that is the length of one short edge plus one long edge of the kite. Tie one end of the string around the top of the kite. Make a loop one-third of the way down the length of the kite frame and knot it. Tie the other end to the bottom of the kite. Trim off any leftover string.

8. To make the tail, use a length of string about five times the height of the kite. Take scraps of paper of about 2 x 3 inches and tie them along the tail string. Attach the tail to the frame.

9. Tie one end of the ball of string to the loop in the bridle.

10. You can be creative like the Kang boys by drawing on the kite or decorating the tail. Now your kite is ready to fly!

## Kite Safety:

1. Don't fly a kite in a thunderstorm or in the rain.
2. Don't fly a kite near electric wires or trees.
3. Don't fly a kite on a busy street or a steep slope.
4. Don't run backwards when launching a kite.
5. Best wear your tennis shoes.

# 作者寄语

风筝起源于中国。中国古代哲学家墨翟在 2400 年前放了一只可能是世界上的第一只风筝。后来，风筝从那里传播到其他亚洲国家，直到全球各地。

没有确切的记录说明风筝是如何或为何而被发明的。通常认为风筝的灵感来自风吹走草帽或飞鸟。风筝具有特别的象征性，因为中国人相信灵魂就像一只飞鸟。人们相信飞在天上的风筝可以赶走天上的邪恶并保护人们的灵魂。

今日的中国，人们放风筝来庆祝节日。在元宵节、春节和秋天的重阳节期间，全国各地的人们通常会在地势较高的地方放风筝，

风筝种类繁多。有些载着小蜡烛灯笼，有些则载着烟火在空中绽放。在众多的品种当中，最有特色的就是带乐器的了。一种风筝吊着贻贝壳，在风中发出咔嗒咔嗒的响声。另一种是顶上带有一只鼓和钹。还有的载着竹笛，在风中发出像竖琴一样的声音。

风弹奏这些风筝犹如音乐家在筝上弹奏一首永无休止的摇篮曲一样。因此，中文"风筝"的"筝"与乐器"筝"的"筝"是同一个字，就像康家兄弟们当初称呼的一样。

## 如何放风筝:

1. 站在地势高的地方，例如山上。在放风筝前计划好奔跑的方向。

2. 背着风向，将风筝拿到空中。当风吹的时候放开风筝，转身逆风尽力奔跑。当你感觉到风在拉扯风筝的时候将绳放长一点，让风帮助你把风筝吹到天上。每当你觉得绳子被拉扯的时候，就把绳子放长些。你会在练习中进步。

# 自制钻石形风筝

在大人的帮助下，你可以按照以下步骤制作风筝。

## 你需要的材料：

- 两根长棒或自制的筷子。请大人帮忙把一根长棍剪成另一根棍子长短的三分之二(例如12英寸和18英寸)
- 一把小刀
- 一卷绳子

- 剪刀
- 胶水或软米饭
- 一大张纸——尝试使用报纸、白纸或你的旧数学作业本
- 一枝马克笔

## 指示：

1. 将短棍的中心点放在长棍的三分之一的地方，形成一个十字。

2. 用绳绕过交叉点三次(从两个方向)，绑一个结，用胶水固定绳结。

3. 请大人帮忙用刀在每枝棍的两端刻上凹痕。

4. 从长棍的底部开始，将绳子放在凹痕里，以顺时针方向通过四个凹痕，拉紧形成钻石形状。绳的尾端应回到长棍的底部。用双结固定绳子。剪掉多余的绳子，或把它留下做尾巴。

5. 把做好的骨架放在纸上。在纸边缘1英寸处画上记号，剪纸。

6. 剪裁好纸张后，将胶水涂在纸的边缘。轻轻把骨架按在纸上，用纸边包起绳框。

7. 制作繮 (连接风筝骨架与风筝线的绳子)，需要剪一条跟风筝的短边和长边加起来一样长的绳子。将绳子的一端绑在风筝的顶部。在风筝骨架往下三分之一的位置绕一个圈并打结。将绳的另一端绑在风筝的下方。剪掉多余的绳子。

8. 制作风筝的尾巴，用一条比风筝长五倍的绳子。将大约2×3英寸的纸粘在用做尾巴的绳子上。将制作好的尾巴粘在骨架上。

9. 将绳子的一端绑在繮的绳环上。

10. 你可以和康家兄弟一样在风筝上画画或装饰风筝的尾巴。现在你的风筝可以放飞了！

## 安全提示：

1. 不要在雷雨天或雨中放风筝。
2. 不要在电线或树旁放风筝。
3. 不要在烦忙的街上或陡坡上放风筝。

4. 不要在放风筝时往后跑。
5. 最好穿运动鞋。

# Enjoy more adventures by the Author!

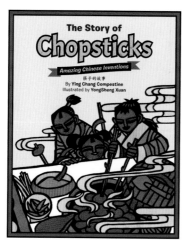

"Like the hues in a stained glass window, [the colors] look brilliant...this well-designed book will please children in the primary grades..."

— *ALA Booklist*

"Kids will love seeing how the antics of the three boys fit with these inventions."

— The Logonauts

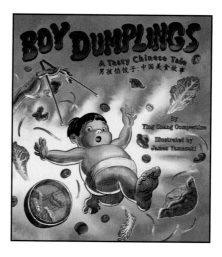

"Compestine's almost tongue-in-cheek tale is a nearly unbeatable combination of slapstick humor, fast pace, and food."

— *The Bulletin of the Center for Children's Books*

"Children will delight in the ghost's gullibility... Compestine's haunting tale is an entertaining, not-too-scary offering..."

— *Publishers Weekly*